Fy and Aina

A New World Love Story

Norse Trollology Series
Book 2

Fy and Aina

A New World Love Story

Written and Illustrated by
Jan Smith

The most salient facts, events and circumstances set forth in this book are the events related to Norse trolls and troll legends. Events are recounted as truthfully as possible using Norse mythology to the limits of the author's perception and ability. Elaborations to enhance readability do not compromise any main truths.

Acknowledgements

Fy from the first book in this series seemed so lonesome to me when his two Nisse friends (trolls), Svart and Liten, went off to find relatives they knew had come over from the Old Country as they did with Fy. Aina enters Fy's life in a dramatic way. What could be better than "saving" a Fjeld troll just his size from drowning to spurn a love affair and companionship in a harsh new world!

Oh, yes, the troll stories promised in the first book of the **NORSE TROLL SERIES, Book 1: Crossing the Arctic** about Fy and his ventures to come to the New World with the two Nisse will be written. **Noki, Lange-Nissen, Tusselader, Tobi-Tre-Fot,** and **Tann-Verk-Trollet** will intrude in the lives of Fy and Aina. Though these troll imposers are all much smaller in size and stature than Fy and Aina, their cavorting and havoc will disrupt and sometimes cause stress and pain. It is my way of recognizing how large people can be bullied too into events and actions and need to be aware of what alternatives they have to combat such behavior short of violence.

Because I am a storyteller, I take liberty in enhancing the Norse legends of yore to create plausible characters for our generation, particularly our young people, so that the stories once told to us or our ancestors continue to live in the hearts of all. I always start my stories with what is historically researched and then add dimension as needed.

I am indebted to my husband who spurs me on when I seem brain-dead for ideas, adds needed elements to incidents I have written, and edits the final product. How lucky I am to have a proof reader right under my own roof!

Chapter 1

"Shoot! Missed him again," Aina said as the lush pink Salmon raced away from the hollowed out log she used as a boat to travel the swift waters of the New World shore. Fishing was wonderful here at the base of the mountain where the stream ran freely into the ocean. Keeping the make-shift canoe-shaped log on course was not easy for her alone in this wilderness area. Big as she was, for she was a mountain troll, Aina still found surviving demanding in this harsh land. Noisy magpies flew from their domed nests above and followed her down the path of the mountainside. Each awaited any morsel escaping from the bait Aina used. They anticipated the leavings after the caught fish were cleaned.

"May, may may!" rang in her ears and "Yak, yak, yak!" made her wish she had her slingshot by her side. She'd make an end to their noise and have meat for the stew pot as well.

Too young to remember her father when he left on one of Leif Erikson's boats, Aina wondered if others had come like he had. Father had hauled many timbers from the top of the mountain down to the Nordic camp here in the New World, adding to the original campsite that Erik Thorvaldson, Leif's father, began ten years before Erik came. Once the camp was completed, Father's indenture was paid. He had not returned to the Old Country and Aina wondered often about him. Harsh winters and a lung illness had sickened Aina's mother, leaving her alone. Lucky was she that her father, before he left, insisted Aina learn to hunt, trap, fish and survive the elements. She was their only child. Little did she know that it would cushion her for the future. Most days she was content here in the New World though she was always lonely.

"Waves are getting stronger," Aina said to the wind. Paddling her boat away from the base of the stream

as it gushed forth, Aina found that the waves were even more intense here than she expected and she struggled to move back, closer to shore and safety. The simple wood paddles she'd carved from another fallen tree were little help. Drifting further out to sea and fearful of being swept away from land by the ever increasing waves, Aina hollered, "*Hjelpe* (help)!" Why, she didn't know. She hadn't seen anyone else since the last boat of Norsemen stopped two months ago. None of the men who came ashore then even knew she was here as she viewed them from her loft above, protected in its own way by natural cover of mountain brush. All returned to the four sailing ships once their barrels were filled with water from the cool, clear stream that flowed down from the mountain top and often served as her shower, cold as that water was coming from the ice caps above. In panic she hollered, louder this time, " *Hjelpe!*" The sea answered her as it rolled one more time and then it happened. Over she went into the frigid waters. Even at her height – for she was as tall as most oak trees – she couldn't stand or reach bottom to push herself up for air. Wave motion sucked the boots she'd made off her feet as the salt water labored to raise her body up. With her head above water, she screamed "*HJELPE!*" as forcefully as she could before the waves rushed over her sinking her again.

Up on the nether side of the cliff Fy, another mountain troll who was busy picking mushrooms for supper, and two Nisse he had brought with him from Norway when he decided to leave his homeland and walk across to the New World, heard the plea as it echoed up across the cliffs to where he stood. Was it possible? Was there someone else here? It had been six months since he had first set foot on this shore. Since then, the waters had risen. Many of the ice floes that he'd used for stepping stones had melted and the sea was rougher. Not thinking what his quick movement would mean to the loose rocks and trees around him, Fy lumbered down the mountain as fast as his Fjeld troll body could move to see who was in need of his help. Rocks and rubble followed, shook loose as his weight made the earth tremble. Fy saw the make-shift wooden canoe first, capsized and washed ashore. Where was its owner? The rough waters made visibility poor. And then – one more time the sea coughed up Aina's body a distance from shore. Fy now knew. Shedding his outer clothing, he lumbered into the icy waters as far out as he could walk and began to swim to where he last saw the body. Once there, he dove, grabbed what he thought was an arm and forced his way to the surface. Struggling with his own huge weight and that of this person, he started back to shore. Gasping for air each time he surfaced enough with the fight to keep the body and himself afloat, he tired quickly in the rough

surf. He swam as best he could with the waves, which he knew would eventually force him to shore or to where he could reach bottom and stand.

Another wave came from behind and pushed both bodies to sand and shore. Wasting little time, Fy fought to stand and dragged what he knew now was a woman much the same size as he onto a sandy area away from the washing waves. Could it be? A soul mate? A companion?   Was she still alive?

Watching a rescue similar to this one where someone had been swept overboard from a fishing boat once when the Norsemen had pulled a body from the sea in the Old Country, Fy used the same tactics. Flipping the lady onto her stomach and placing her head to the side, he straddled her legs, leaned forward and pushed on the area just below the shoulder blades. Then he lifted her body at the hips, laid her down flat again and pushed once more. This time water spewed out of her mouth as she gasped for air. Fy slid off her legs as she began to stir, coughing and panting. Gently, he helped her to roll over, cradling her head in his hands and propping it on his thigh as he brushed the hair away from her face. Eyes fluttered open. "Rest," Fy said. "You are safe with me." Svart and Liten, the two Nisse who had come with Fy and had used his shoulders and head as transportation to this New World, cheered. They'd hurried to try scramble away from the falling rock and debris, loosened when Fy hurried down the mountain. Following behind and navigating the chaos in their small steps, the two watched in awe as life came back to the lady Fy had pulled from the waters. "Need a fire," Fy said to the two of them in a kind but desperate voice and off they scampered, ready to help.

Dragging bits and pieces of driftwood, sometimes as big as they were and using dried sea weed, the two scuttled and struggled until they had a pile as tall as they.

Handing Fy a tinder box the two always kept in their knapsack, he reached towards the fire while disturbing the lady as little as possible and struck two stones together that caused enough spark to start the tinder at the base of the pile. Soon all was in flame and heat filled the air.

Aina sensed the heat and stirred, opened her eyes and gazed into the most beautiful face she had seen in a long time. Could it be? Another Fjeld mountain troll here in this new land? Still soaked from her ordeal but wanting to sit up and get closer to the fire to warm herself, she carefully rolled to her side and was helped to a sitting position.

"Are you hurt?" Fy asked her with concern on his face.

"Only my pride," Aina said, dropping her head in shyness. "How could you know a big roller was coming, big enough to dump you overboard? Were you fishing?"

"The salmon are running and I love dried salmon. I ate the last of my dried fish last night and need to restock." Embarrassed, Aina said, "The boat has never failed me before."

"How long have you been here?" Fy asked.

"Two years. I came as a slave with one of the Norsemen as the galley cook. Torger promised freedom if I would come." Aina was silent for a while and then said. "He was true to his word. He left me when they went back."

"Are there others here?"

"No. I have seen no one, not even any Nisse here," she said as she smiled at the two who were listening. "I've been lonely."

"Where do you live?" asked Fy, wondering if she were strong enough yet to even stand.

"Up there," Aina pointed. "See that rock sticking out? There's a cave there. Varg is usually at my side. He must be hunting too."

"Varg? Who's he? I thought you said you were alone," replied Fy with disappointment in his voice.

"I am. Varg is a wolf that came one night. His paw was bleeding. Looked like he'd been caught in some kind of trap. I patched it up as much as he would let me and he's been with me ever since." Smiling shyly Aina said, "He often brings hares and fox for my stewpot."

"I think the fire has dried most of our clothing. How about if I walk with you back to your cave? I'd offer to take you to mine but I know that my running down the trail caused rocks and trees to tumble behind me. I've work to do before the trail is clear again, I'm sure." The two Nisse were quick to agree.

"I can make it on my own," Aina said in a stern, take charge voice. She stood and then realized how weak she really was as she staggered. Smiling, Aina said, "I guess I'd better not be so proud and let you help. It's a long climb up."

Together they walked side by side, resting when either one needed. Fy too was tired from fighting the current and waves. The Nisse stayed behind and doused the fire, not an easy task for their small bodies.

Chapter 2

Six days passed slowly for Fy as he recalled the events of the rescue. Returning from Aina's, Fy'd picked up each Nissen in his hands, and carefully placed them on his shoulders again. Each hung on to beard or hair so as not to tumble off. He'd lumbered cautiously back up the path to his cave home, diligently setting aside debris that cluttered the path up the mountainside.

Fy woke each morning, looked across to the mountainside where he knew Aina's cave was, hoping to catch sight of her. Each day brought more disappointment.   Her boat remained where it had washed ashore and she didn't come to use it.

"She must be lonely," Fy said to no one. He was lonesome too. The Nisse had taken their rucksacks filled with food and their tools, determined to see where their ancestors had gone. Each knew that Nisse had hidden in Norsemen's trunks or in part of the boat's rigging, hitching rides that way to the New World. Seeking adventure was foremost in their lives. Torger, much older than they, had told them others had come before when they'd asked for advice just before the two left on the journey to the New World. A group of Nisse had snagged a ride with Leif Erikson on his boat without him knowing it when he first came here about ten years ago. That's why they were anxious to come with Fy. Some who came with Leif were relatives.

When his two small friends left, Fy wanted to help them and did. Never sure what roamed in the tall grasses, he knew animals lurking would harm them as they crossed the valley to the forest beyond. He was determined to send them safely on their way by placing them on his shoulders and walked with them across the marsh and grass to the other side and the forest.

Mockingbirds singing "May! May!" announced their progress. Protective Fy, determined to ease their journey, carried the Nisse through the valley and grass that reached his waist.

"Ouch!" Svart said as his head hit Fy's ear when Fy stepped in a hole made by some animal. A deer scared out of its bedded down area bounded off as each flat-footed step Fy made shook the ground.

"Hurt much?"

"No. Did I pull your hair too hard?"

"I felt a twitch, nothing more," was Fy's reassurance.

Once to the nether side, Fy walked to a tree with a hollow in its branches that looked like it could be their home for this night. He allowed the Nisse to clamber into the crook. While placing the two on a low tree branch, Fy sighed and a tear slid down his cheek. He'd miss their help doing the little things his big hands and body made difficult.

Using their hatchets, Svart and Liten secured themselves in the crook. Each thanked the other for time spent together. Trees, caves and barn lofts had always been home for the Nisse. Svart and Liten felt safe here, even if this forest area was new to them. Hollows in trees or tunnels made by the roots had served as protection when needed in the Old Country and would now, they knew, as they began this venture to find relatives.

Carefully taking his little finger and gently rubbing the top of each head, Fy said, "Thanks for your company on this journey to the New World. Sorry about the whale ride. I know you were scared and so was I part of the time. You know where to find me if you need help. If you see any more Fjeld trolls, let them know that Aina and I are here too," and he turned and walked back across the grassland toward his cave. Another tear slid down his cheek. These two had nursed him when he was sick. They were true friends.

Returning to his cave went quicker. Fy could take longer strides since the Nisse were not on his shoulders. He headed towards the mountain base through the same high grasses. It wasn't long as he walked and something rubbed his hand. Reaching down cautiously, he sensed an animal, turned to the side and saw a wolf. "Varg?" he questioned as he scratched the area between its ears.

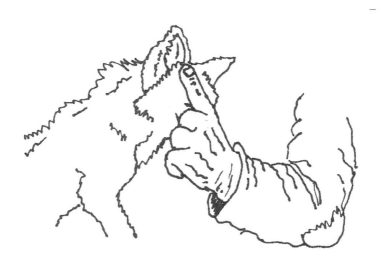

Though comforted by the wolf's easy companionship, his mind was cluttered and he wondered what to do now to break the loneliness and need with the Nisse gone. They were true friends who had helped him do chores that his size made somewhat impossible to do. His eyes roved to the other side as he walked, to where he knew Aina lived. Why was wolf here? Was she well? Time for a visit, he thought, but first he had work to do.

Chapter 3

Morning dawned cool and clear. The sun shone with promise of a warm, spring day. Fy took the largest cedar basket that the Nisse had made for him, piled shingle-like pieces into it, placed it on his shoulder and moved along the side trail he'd found that ran between his cave and Aina's. He used the upper handle of the spear as a walking stick to balance himself along the uneven trail. If the salmon were running, Fy knew that the brook and pool not far away would be full of orange-yellow fish ready for the taking. The Nisse had discovered this prized fishing hole on one of their treks.

Fish. Filet them. Put them in the basket. Bring Aina the salmon filets as a surprise. That was the plan. She could eat them as she wanted or keep them for winter storage.

Gingerly Fy stepped his way along the trail. Small loose boulders were a bother and Fy avoided them, hoping not to lose his balance and tumble back down through the brush and trees as he had done just before his journey here. The Old Country tumble had cost him a knock on his head but the Nisse were good and helped him recover.

And then it happened. Again! Fy stepped on what he thought was a solid, flat rock and it teetered, causing his huge bulky body to lose its balance and lunge forward. Landing, Fy hit his shoulder first and then he rolled like a log until a tree stopped the downhill plunge. The basket went flying. So did the spear he used as a walking stick and impaled itself on a tree, just missing a hare that was out for a stroll. He clutched his shoulder. The echoes of "Ouch, that hurts!" railed in the air. Fy's landing was beside a large cedar tree, and he remained splayed out and unconscious much like the last time it happened in the Old Country.

Aina, just rising for the day, went to her usual ledge to comb the snarls from her hair creating two braids to hang alongside her cheeks. The cry came echoing up the mountainside. "Fy!," she though. "What happened? Oh, my . . ." she too wailed as she scurried, struggling through brush and briar to find the source of the plaintive yowl. Down she moved with Varg by her side, ever closer to the moans. Then she saw him at the base of the mountainside, lying still, with his hand clutching his shoulder. Quickly, taking a good sized leaf off a tree, she fashioned a cup, scooped water from the brook nearby and brought it to his lips. The first attempt she made was unsuccessful. Water ran down his chin, around his neck and on the ground. Returning to the brook, she fashioned another leaf cup, scooped more water and this time used it to wet his brow, hoping that the cool water would awaken him and it did. Using the hand of the uninjured arm as a towel, Fy wiped water away from his chin. "I . . . did it . . . again" were the first words Fy slowly uttered.

"What do you mean, 'You did it again'?"

Groggily in slow faltering words Fy answered, "I slipped . . . just before I walked across . . . to come here from the Old Country. That time I hit . . . my head very hard. This time I think I have hurt . . . my shoulder," Fy mumbled through the pain as he used the other hand to massage the area. "It's a good thing I didn't fall on my spear . . . or I would be a dead troll," Fy added, still mumbling. "Do you see it or my basket?"

"What spear? What basket? I don't see anything around here but you," Aina responded in a soothing voice. "Rest a while. I will get you some more water and then we will talk," she said as she left him to find more leaves suitable for making a cup.

"No, don't bother," Fy mumbled. "I'll be . . ." but she was already gone.

Fy shifted his body into a better position, more comfortable than that of his fall. Aina came rushing towards him. "She is so beautiful," he mouthed quiet enough so she wouldn't hear, awe-struck with her beauty. Her hair was combed, braided and held back by vines entwined to secure them. Her dress

was of the softest deerskin he'd ever
seen.

                              Coming
closer she knelt by him and
offered more water which he did

sip. Sitting on her haunches at his side, out of curiosity she asked, unsure that she had heard right, "You had a spear and a basket? What were you gathering or hunting? Are you rested enough to talk or should we wait a while?"

"It will be my surprise," is all he would say and dozed off.

Realizing that he probably did need rest, Aina left him and scrambled back to her cave. As quickly as she could she ladled some broth from the pot always filled with some kind of food. It continuously hung over her hearth in the middle of the cave. The bowl was one she had carved from some cedar. Moving quickly but carefully so as not to spill the bowl's contents, Aina found her way back to the still sleeping giant. "Fy," she said in her normal-toned voice. He didn't move. "Fy," she repeated, louder this time, hoping he would wake. He did not. Worried now, Aina set the bowl down, and reached over and nudged him, forgetting that the shoulder she nudged was the one he had hurt.

Waking, Fy yowled in pain and sat up, forcing Aina backward and spilling the broth in the bowl.

"Now you've done it," she said in an irritable voice. "Guess you aren't as hurt as I thought you were."

Reaching for her in a cumbersome way and touching her hand, Fy said, "I'm sorry. I'm always so clumsy. Forgive me," and he hung his head as he clutched his shoulder.

"Wait here. I'll get more broth and some wrapping for your shoulder," Aina encouraged. "I think it's best you don't use it for a day or two until it heals a little." Off she ran once again as best as her Fjell troll size would allow her. Fy could feel the rumbling of the ground as she moved and he smiled through the pain. A soul mate crossed his mind again as he leaned back against the tree waiting for her return.

Rain came in torrents for the next three long days. Fy spent the time repairing the retrieved basket as well as he could. How he wished those two little Nisse were here. They'd have the basket rewoven in no time. Aina'd found it impaled on a tree branch. One puncture hole – repairable with some careful weaving.

Welcoming sunshine on the fourth day brought Fy out of his doldrums. Grabbing the basket and spear, he headed back to the brook, hoping the weather had not chased his catches away. "Yak, yak, yak" followed him. The magpies knew his plan too! Yellow-gold splashing greeted him when he got to the pool. Seven thrusts of the spear reaped seven huge lush salmon. Gutting them was easy. Carrying them back to his cave to smoke took time. His body still complained of the pain from the fall.

Back at the cave, Fy arranged the half slabs of salmon meat on the racks he had fashioned above the fire pit, made just for the purpose of curing meat. He scurried to gather more dry cedar before nightfall, knowing the fire would need tending all night if the meat was to cure. Fish smoked quickly but the fire needed to be constant. He couldn't wait to see the smiles on Aina's face when he brought her the surprise.

Chapter 4

Phew! What was that smell? Aina woke with a start, realizing something was not right. Rotten meat! That's what it was. How could it be? She had eaten most of what she had cured. The last hare she snagged with a sling shot she'd finished off last night before sleeping. Cautiously, Aina arose, dressing quickly without fussing with her hair. Moving closer to the cave entrance she found Varg lying crossways in the entrance as he usually did – protection for her.

"Phew!" He *was* the answer! The wind was blowing in to the entrance and with it came the smell. Varg's greatest thrill seemed to be feasting on a kill, leaving what he was not able to eat for other animals. All that was good and fine but he also loved to return in a week's time or so and roll in the remains. Why? Aina had no answer!

"Rmhf," Varg rumbled as he rolled over on his side to be scratched.

"Where have you been?" she asked.

"Rmhf," was his reply.

A shower had not been in her plans for today but Varg gave her no choice. Gathering a clean set of leggings and shirt, the soap she had made from tallow and crushed pine needles, a bowl, a larger piece of leather she used as a towel and her comb that her mother had given her long ago made from a carved seal tusk, Aina moved toward the entrance and called Varg to her side as she made her way down the mountainside to the shore where the small waterfall she used as a shower flowed freely.

The walk down the trail to the ocean shore was uneventful. Seeing the boat left on the bank, Aina reminded herself to check if there had been damage. She was most concerned about the oars. Carving them had taken her some time and she still needed to fish salmon before the cold set in and ice covered the shore as far out as she could see.

Hesitating some to step into the waterfall knowing how cold the water was coming from the ice flow above, she stood first with only her feet in the water as she soaped and rinsed the clothing she's removed. Satisfied the pieces were as clean as she could get them, she called Varg to her. He stood close to her but would not get into the water. Taking the bowl, Aina used it to ladle water onto Varg's fur.

Unused to a bath, Varg tried to scurry away but Aina hung on to him, grabbing onto the fur just behind the ears. Once she had him wet, she rubbed him with the same soap she used for clothes washing and her bathing. Soap. Water. Soap. Water. Soap. Water. Three times she repeated the process and each time Varg became less tolerant. When she let go, he scampered and shook, scampered and shook again, glad to be rid of the strange feeling of the bath.

"My turn," she spoke. Using the bowl, Aina poured water over her head, lathered the soap in and then bravely stepped into the downward flow of the waterfall. Toweling off as much as she could, she waited a bit to "air dry" more, put her clean clothes on and sat on a nearby ledge gazing out to sea. Combing her hair was always a chore but it was soothing too.

The sea appeared calm today, not like the day the boat had capsized. Could she take it out again even on a day like this where there were few waves? Fear shot through her but she knew if she were to survive the winter, she needed food. Her greatest love was salmon. The only way to get them that she knew of was to take the boat out and fish. "I better check the boat," she thought as she hopped off the ledge. Reaching the craft, Aina saw that the boat was intact and no worse for wear.

"But the oars . . . where have they gone," Aina softly wailed.

Lumbering her way, Aina moved up and down the shoreline hoping to find them. The lone woman realized that she was in trouble, trouble she had not faced before. Food. All summer long she'd dried berries and harvested roots suitable to eat. What she had stored for the winter would not last her she knew. She could hunt hares, magpies and other birds with her slingshot. What she really needed was a good supply of meat. Close to tears and with darkness looming on the horizon, Aina started back up the trail to her cave, saddened by the work she had ahead of her to accomplish winter survival in this harsh land.

Chilled to the bone from the raging winds that blew in her face as Aina moved up the trail after her shower, she struggled up the mountainside. This Nor'easter was the same wind that upended her boat when she fished for salmon. Anxious to be protected from it, Aina was glad to see the entrance and hurried to the hearth when she got inside the cave, sat on the closest rock near the fire pit that was her chair and rubbed her hands to warm them.

As she warmed, she relaxed though her body shook with chills still. Paying more attention to her surroundings, she sniffed.

"Oh my, what is *that* smell?", she queried. Moving to the hearth with some hesitation, she took a bowl and reached for the ladle to taste the contents in the pot. Had she been so addled by Varg's terrible odor that she forgot what she had in the kettle?

"But it was empty!" She remembered she'd placed the cleaned pot on the side of the hearth, ready to start something fresh to eat this morning.

"Mmmm!" The contents were good! Who could have made it? Looking around, Aina spotted other changes. The few clothes she had were neatly hung on pegs along the wall. Her pallet was straightened. The small wood stump she used as a table looked like it had been polished clean. Had Fy come back? Would he just come in, make himself at home, and clean? Aina didn't think so. Most troll men would *never* do woman's work. But who? Tired from the trek to bathe and the burden she now had of replacing the oars, Aina went to bed, covered herself with the warm bearskin blanket hoping to shake off the chills and slept. It had been a long and eventful day.

Two small Nisse, Hans and Tina, stirred off a hidden ledge from their lofty spot in the far corner of the cave. As quietly as they could, the two came down and took the bowl and spoon Aina had used. Tina washed them in the wood basin close to the fire and Hans struggled but finally got them on the shelf where the rest of the cooking utensils were. "I'm going out to find more kindling," Hans said as quietly as he could trying not to disturb Aina's rest.

"I'll get these nuts ground and mix some fry bread for morning. I put some Hyssop in the stew she had earlier today. That should allow her to rest peacefully and heal. Be careful for the wolf," was Tina's warning as Hans went out the cave entrance.

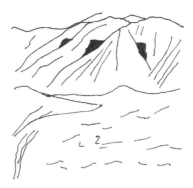

Chapter 5

"They're dry," Fy stated with the authority of one who had experience as he tested the meatiest parts of one salmon filet for doneness. Satisfied the fish was well cured, he grinned and added, "Time to deliver my surprise."

Off came the basket from the wall and in went the smoked filets. Fy hoisted the heavy basket on his *good* shoulder and took his spear down from the wall to use as a cane to balance himself as he walked.

In the weeks since he'd been hurt and last seen Aina, Fy had explored more of the mountainside. With some hard labor made even more difficult because of his shoulder, he'd moved some rocks, a tree or two, and various brushes overgrowing the walkway. He'd cleared a cross trail which wove around part of the mountain. The new trail section now connecting to the old still appeared to the eye as a hopeless slope to negotiate. Fy'd discovered a hole large enough for him to pass through that had been made over the course of time by the rushing of waters coming down from above. The hole had led to another softer ridge, comfortable enough to accommodate his movement as it wound around the mountainside to Aina's cave.

Fy used his new trail now, hoping to get to deliver his surprise by midday. Taking the original trail would mean a day down the side of the mountain, across a little valley tucked

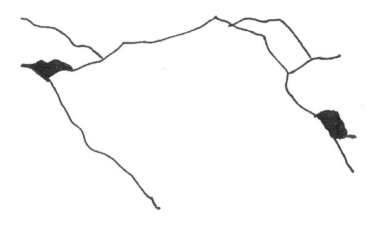

between the two mountains and then up her side of the mountain. Even with his size and strides, he would have difficulty reaching her before late day. He was especially anxious to show her the catch. He'd worked hard to establish this new trail and he didn't think she'd have discovered it yet.

Fy'd deliberately left some brush at the very spot where the two trails met going up on her side to disguise its presence.

"I must walk very carefully," he uttered aloud, "specially with the burdensome weight of this basket." The fresh, new footpath still was hazardous in its own way. Loose rock and ground not settled by use or rains made a precarious venture for Fy's big feet! The spear helped to balance his stride but the sharp stone edge of the blade often came close to his face as it shifted on the softened earth.

"She's so beautiful and I'm so lonely all the time now that the Nisse are gone," was all Fy could think as he stopped at the joining section of the

old trail just ahead of the ledge that
reached her cave. As he gazed up to

her entrance above and the ledge
beside, he saw Aina sitting on a boulder
combing the snarls out of her long hair.

The sun shone on her back. The leather dress she wore now was decorated with beads and dye.

"Where did she learn those leather skills?" Fy wondered with envy as he looked down at his feet. His shoes were a sorry sight! He'd taken an extra skin he'd cured from hunting hares and carefully cut it to make a liner for each shoe's sole area. He knew it wouldn't be long and the patchwork would come through the holes. He'd need replacements or he'd have to go barefoot. How he missed the Nisse! They'd made his first pair of New World shoes.

"I wonder if she can make shoes. I can barter more salmon, and maybe some magpie eggs," Fy thought to himself.

Unaware of Fy's doting eyes, Aina began to sing.

Time waits for no one.
Life takes its toll.
Memories what's left
For this mountain troll.
Heaven's reward
Waits for us all.
We must believe
In salvation for all.

"You have a beautiful voice," Fy offered walking closer and impulsively ducked as a rock came flying by his ear.

"Oh!" Aina wailed. She'd reached instinctively for her slingshot which was usually by her side for just such protection, grabbed a small rock also at ready, and fired as she turned to defend herself from whoever was approaching. Scrambling off the boulder as quickly as her size could muster, she blubbered with tears in her eyes and fear in her voice, "Did I hurt you?"

"No, you missed. Good thing I was watching you or you wouldn't have. You are very good with that sling."

"I think I told you that my per (father) made sure I could take care of mor (mother) and myself before he left with Leif. I practice daily either in the cave or out here to keep my skills honed. If I wouldn't have been singing, you wouldn't have sneaked up so close," Aina said with pride in her voice. "How did you get here? You didn't come up the lower trail. I would have seen you." And then she spied the basket. Coming closer, she whispered. "Is that my surprise? What's in the basket? How did you get here?" Aina mouthed, grinning from ear to ear.

"So many questions," teased Fy. "Since I last saw you, I've discovered and cleared a new trail that goes over the crags in a round about way from my cave to you. We don't have to go down and up the mountain any more."

"That's why I didn't see you come," Aina exclaimed with more comfort in her demeanor, feeling that her awareness to intruders was still intact.

"You'll have to sit on that boulder with your back to your entrance," Fy chided. "From now on you'll have two directions to watch if you don't want unannounced company." With worry in his voice, Fy uttered, " I didn't think about that as I cleared a trail so that we could get together easier."

"So what's in the basket? Looks like you've repaired it well. Did the Nisse come back?"

"More questions and I haven't answered the others yet," Fy cajoled. "The Nisse didn't come back, "Fy said with a bit of sadness in his voice, again looking at his shoes. "I often watched them weave so I had some idea of what to do."

"Please, Fy," Aina pleaded. "What's my surprise? No one has surprised me for so long that I have no patience, I know. I'm like a small child."

Walking over to the ledge that served as a lookout as well as a *chair* outside, Fy emptied the basket's contents and stood back. Her reaction was one of comfort and joy. Pride filled his heart as he watched awe spread across Aina's face.

"Salmon! Oh, my! Salmon!" Aina whispered and then began to dance around forcing her large frame to move. "And smoked! Ready for winter – IF they last that long!" she said with embarrassment. "I haven't had even a morsel for so long. My mouth is watering already."

"Eat your fill. There is more in the pool not far from here where these came from."

Aina's ears perked. "What do you mean pool? Not far? These didn't come from the ocean below?"

"Have you explored around here very much?"

"I'm brave but not foolish," was her reply. "Being alone and a woman is not easy. I have skills but I am cautious."

"I probably wouldn't have found the pool either if the Nisse hadn't discovered it." The two who had come with him often left their home in Fy's cave for the night and came back in the early morning, saddened, but filled with news of their finds. The pool was one such discovery. Who would have thought he'd missed them so much.

"The pool . . ." Aina prompted disturbing Fy's daydreaming.

"Questions! Questions! More questions! Thank those Nisse again!" Fy said. "They discovered the pool the week we were first here after our journey from the Old Country. They were roaming the area looking for some of their relatives. That pool has been a treasure for me often."

"Not far from here? Will you show it to me? I know – more questions. I'm sorry. I have been alone for so long. It's a wonder I still know how to talk," Aina said, smiling as she humbly bent her head and looked at him.

"Of course I'll show you. First, have a treat," Fy said, offering Aina one of the smaller pieces that had broken off a filet slab. Fy watched as Aina ate, licking her fingers as she savored each bite.

"Smoked to perfection and salted just right!" Aina declared. "How can I repay you? I know, another question but I was taught to return favors. I'll need more salmon for the winter. Maybe we could work together. But I still want to do something for you," Aina pleaded with pride in her voice and her mind running rampant.

Both had been sitting on the same ledge where Fy first saw Aina earlier. Fy had without thinking raised one foot and curled it under his other for comfort. Without meaning to, he inadvertently exposed the worn condition of his shoe's sole.

"Is this the only pair of shoes you have?" Aina asked with concern in her voice, knowing the harsh, cold winter was soon approaching.

"With the Nisse gone. . . I have more skins . . ." was all Fy could think to say.

"How about shoes for salmon?" Aina offered with tenderness in her voice as she placed a hand on his knee.

"Deal!" Fy agreed and reached for her hand to shake it, feeling a pulsing emotion as he did. Could this be? A life mate? His heart sang.

The heated aura between them evaporated as Varg leaped down from above, stuck his nose between them, and "Rmhf"ed, wanting to be a part of their togetherness.

Chapter 6

"What have you?" Tina questioned Hans as he dragged two large objects behind him.

"Sheep horns, I think," offered Hans. "Haven't seen any drinking gourds around the cave like we had back in the Old Country. Thought Aina might like to have these and not have to use those leaves all the time. How is she?"

"Her body is so hot. Being so chilled by the water when she fell overboard into the sea must have made her ill."

"Her mother was always ill. My mor told me she cared for Gilda many times. Aina was too small to remember I am sure," Hans recalled.

"Good thing we hitched a ride in Aina's trunk when she came as a servant. She has needed us many times," was Tina's observation.

"She still doesn't sense we are here, does she?"

"No, but she is getting curious now that I have started to make stew."

"What shall I do with the horns?" wondered Hans. "They need cleaning before they can be used."

"Let's put them behind the trunk. She has not looked there in a long time." Tina took the makeshift broom Hans had made for her from a soft brush that grew on the mountainside, covered the tracks made from dragging the horns, and scurried back into the shadows of the cave as Aina stirred.

"I must really be sick," Aina thought, weakly spooning out a ladleful into her wooden bowl. "I don't remember making this gruel. It has nuts in it. Where did I get them?" Aina pondered but all she could do was take three spoonfuls before she was tired again and gingerly went to lie down. "How many days have passed?" she wondered. How she hoped Fy would come for a visit. She was always more lonely when she did not feel well.

"Varg? Is that you?" Aina whispered, too tired to do more. From her sleeping bench covered with the bearskin, Aina could see a large animal shape in the entrance to the cave. "Vang?"

From a ledge above, a rock aimed at the animal's forehead hit its mark and a loud roar of a lion bellowed forth. Just as quickly, three more rocks found their aim. More roars followed along with a retreat of the menacing danger.

Hans scrambled down and made his way to the cave entrance to make sure that the mountain lion had moved off. "I need to protect the women. Aina is ill and Tina is no match for the beast," Hans mumbled out loud as he moved as fast as his small form could to the opening.

Stunned, Aina spoke, "Nisse? In my cave?" Where had they come from? Were these the two that were Fy's friends and they had moved in with her?

Sitting up with great difficulty in her weakened condition, Aina softly spoke. "Who are you? When did you come? What did you scare off?" Then she knew. "YOU made the stews?" Her face shone with radiance, thankful for the company. She knew that if she were good to them, they would always be loyal.

"I'm Hans and this is Tina. We came with you," he quietly stated, pointing to the trunk in the corner of the cave.

"Why me?" Why my trunk?"

"We often cared for your Mor and you when she was sick when your father left and you were still so small," Tina filled in as she walked closer to the sleeping bench where Aina now rested. "We knew Gilda would want us to be with you on this journey."

"All this time – two years, and I never suspected I had company. How can I thank you?"

"First, when you are better, we need to see about that mountain lion that came visiting and see about Varg. Hope he was not last night's dinner for the roaming beast!" replied Hans.

"Wish Fy would come. He could help us. I wonder if I could send Varg as a messenger? Would Fy understand that we need him to come? Do you know where Varg is? Have you seen him? Could he have been hurt? I know. Too many questions again. I am so worried."

Chapter 7

Lumbering on three legs and almost collapsing with each step, Varg came but to the wrong cave. Massive claw marks on the underside of his body oozed blood. One paw was severely maimed and raw. Fy scrambled towards the agonized wolf as it whimpered in intense pain to see how he could help ease the animal's anguish. Too heavy to lift, Fy ran back into his cave and retrieved a deer skin he'd used before when he needed to transport something even his massive body could not handle alone. Placing the skin on the back side of Varg, Fy took the two legs closest to the ground and rolled the wolf onto the skin. "Roooomhf!" in a plaintive wail came from Varg but his eyes pleaded for help. With all his strength, Fy laboriously dragged the skin and wolf into his cave and near the hearth.

Going to his shelf where he kept medicine, Fy found a bowl he had carved with its lid and brought it over to the breath-labored wolf. "Easy, boy," Fy offered as he began to smear a salve he often used on open wounds himself – fat mixed with the yarrow that he'd found in the valley below.

As gently as he could, Fy covered the clawed underbelly of the wolf. Varg somehow sensed he needed to lie still, nor did he growl or whimper.

The paw was another matter. Each time Fy reached to touch the flesh-torn foot, the rmhf's grew stronger. Finally, Fy took the salve and smeared the whole foot in the areas that the animal would allow. Last, Fy offered Varg water. The exhausted wolf licked two laps and collapsed back on the skin.

Convinced that there was little else to do for Varg, Fy ventured out of his cave with sling and spear in his hands.

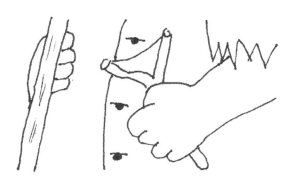

"Let's see if two are wounded," he reasoned with himself. Cautiously, always looking up, Fy searched the immediate area and found no trace of the mountain lion he knew had caused the damage to Varg. His mind raced to Aina. Somehow he needed to warn her of the danger and let her know Varg was here. Darkness came quickly in this **New World** at this time of year and was imminent in the western sky. Reluctantly, Fy retraced his footsteps back to his cave, knowing that he'd have to wait until morning. All he could hope for was that Aina had not gone salmon fishing or berry picking – that she too was not out looking for Varg.

One look as Fy woke from his restless night's sleep told him that Varg was still lying by the hearth. The wolf had moved some but still lay on his side with the wounded paw now tucked close to the body.

"Let's see how you are faring," Fy said as he moved towards the animal. "The salve has helped. You're not oozing blood as you were." The paw too appeared less mangled, swollen but intact. "More water?" Fy urged as he placed a shallow wood bowl beside the wolf. With difficulty, Varg drank, and then accepted a piece of dried meat. Strength ebbed and the once vibrant wolf lay again, back on the skin. "You stay here, boy. I'm going to Aina and tell her you're here." The wolf's ears pricked up. "It'll take me most of the day. I'll be back by nightfall. I can't risk being out in dark with that lion about."

Shuffling his way across the new trail, Fy remained always alert to the possibility that he might be leapt on by the maddened and probably wounded lion. Very tired, but so thankful that he'd arrived safely, Fy called as he reached the area where the two trails met.

"Aina." Silence. "Aina! Are you there?" Fy called more sharply with concern in his voice. No answer came. With effort, Fy lumbered the rest of the way to the cave entrance. What met his eyes as he walked into the cave nearly devastated him. There lying on her bench, covered with a simply woven blanket was Aina, unmoving.

"Aina! Aina, what has happened?" Fy pleaded as he rushed to her side. "Are you ill? Are you hurt? What has happened?"

Softly and with difficulty Fy heard, "So . . . many . . questions . . ."

"Oh, my dear, you are alive. I was so worried. I've been alone so long . . ." With that Fy stopped talking, a little embarrassed, realizing he probably shared more than he should have.

"There's . . . stew . . ."

"Are you hungry? Do you have a fever?" and then his mind kicked into gear. "Who made the stew? How long have you been sick?"

"So . . . many . . ." was all Aina said until Fy interrupted her.

"I know. One thing at a time. Are you thirsty?" Fy said as he came back with a ladle of water from the almost empty bucket near the hearth.

With Fy holding her head aright so she could drink, Aina struggled. Collapsing back on her bed of furs, she said, "Why are you" and she paused to cough "here? Did the Nisse find you and tell you to come?"

"Nisse! You mean *my* Nisse are here? I've missed them so."

"Not *your* Nisse. Hans. Tina," Aina called, looking towards the back of the cave. "Please, will you come and meet Fy?"

Softly but with caution, the two came from the loft that was their home. "We came in her chest when she came," explained Hans as he extended his hand to the massive form.

Fy carefully shook the oh-so-small hand and said, "Thanks for taking care of her so well."

"Did you come for a visit? Did you bring more salmon?" blurted out Aina between breaths.

"Varg, " was all Fy said and Aina with difficulty sat up.

"Varg? My wolf Varg? What has happened to him? Did the lion get him?" Sinking back onto the bench with tears streaming down her face, she wept. "I'll miss him so. He was my guardian, my peace of mind."

"Please, Aina. Stop crying, dear. Varg is at my cave."

"Your cave? Why? Why? Why not here?

"He came to me last night just before dark, struggling to move. His right front paw is badly mangled. He has deep scratches from a mountain lion on his underbelly."

"Will he live?"

"Yes, I think so unless infection sets in. I put salve on the wounds that he would let me touch."

"The lion?"

"Still about," Fy cautioned. "I looked for him. I suspect he too is wounded. That's why I came. To warn you."

"I heard him two nights ago, the night I became ill."

"What can I do for you before I go? I need to get back before nightfall. I promised Varg I would."

"Oh, Fy. Is it safe for you? You could stay here and go back in the morning," Aina offered with shyness in her voice.

"Promise me that you will not wander about until we can *together* hunt the lion? Four eyes and two sling shots and my spear are better than trying to hunt alone. Agreed?"

"It will be some days judging by the way I feel before I'll have strength back. I think I've the same chest heaviness that my mother suffered from. Hans' family cared for

Mor. He and Tina will care for me now. I'll get better. Please take care of Varg. He's all I have."

Hesitating somewhat but with a determinedness in his voice, Fy continued, "When you and Varg are both well, the three of us and now Hans and Tina need to make other plans. Fear of you being alone and my losing you has speeded up those plans."

"Plans? You're not going back to the Old Country, are you?" Aina blubbered through tears running down her face at the thought of losing him.

"No, dear. I have better plans than that." Reaching for a drinking gourd Hans had fashioned that now hung on the wall by a leather thong, Fy poured just a little wine from a bladder that hung on the same wall. Tina made excellent berry wines from the endless supply found nearby. Fy drank a small sip and then offered the same to Aina as he

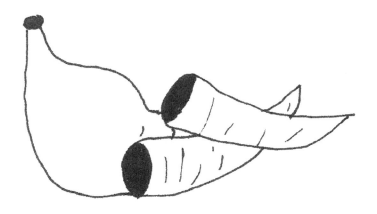

quietly stated with a protectiveness in his voice, "Will you live with me for the rest of our lives?"

Aina's eyes filled with tears but the smile on her face was radiant. The two Nisse cheered as she too sipped and answered, "So many questions. . ." and then giggled.

Norse Trollology Series - Book 1

Crossing the Arctic

by Jan Smith

Crossing the Arctic is the story of a Norse Fjell Trollet, a mountain troll. Ridiculed because of his lack of cleanliness, Fy decides to follow in his father's footsteps and make his way from Norway to the **New World** in order to start a new life for himself. Receded fjord waters impacted by glacial movement and ice jams in the Arctic allow Fy to take advantage of his huge height and *walk* across. Two Nisse, small Norse troll people, accompany him and the three face adventures on the journey to the **New World**.

ORDERING BOOKS

- Place order on website:
  <u>storiesandyou.com</u>

- Books will be shipped media mail –no postage charged to buyer.

CONTACT THE AUTHOR

jansmith@storiesandyou.com

Coming Soon . . .

Noki, a Fishing Troll

Noki doesn't like people fishing in the ocean, lakes and streams. Loves to swipe fishermen's bait and scare fish away.

Lange-Nissen, a Long Nose Troll

Poke wants to be included in everything and in doing so, gets his nose into situations that cause him and others trouble.

Tusselader, a Nuisance Troll

Tussi causes havoc, spoils food, molds bread, hides keys and loves flies.

Tobi-Tre-Fot, Wooden Legged Troll

Tobi lost his leg, grew mean and causes lots of trouble wherever he goes.

Tan-Verk-'Trollet, Toothache Troll

Tann always carries a small hammer and chisel. He constantly looks for a new home and wastes no time using his tools on unsuspecting humans.

Synopsis of Historical Fiction books
written by Jan Smith:

Homesteading the Land
Phelps Mill - 1890

The story is set in Otter Tail County in the
Phelps Mill area known then as Maine,
Minnesota.   Arriving by prairie schooner,
living in a tent, building a sod house and
finally a log home, each become adventures
for Nivek. Almost daily visits to the mill
delivering lunch, to McConkey's store, school
and farming, fishing and hunting (sometimes
with the neighbor boys) become "lessons in
life." **Homesteading the Land** is a fictional
look at the daily life of a land-claiming family
of five in the year 1890.   Many of the
characters, events and places, however,
allude to *actual local people and happenings*
of that year.   *197 pages – author illustrated*

Remembering the Maine
Riding with Roosevelt

Remembering the Maine continues the story of the young Nivek James, introduced in the previous book **Homesteading the Land**. Leaving his family homestead in Minnesota, he becomes a newspaper correspondent during the Spanish-American War, 1898. With his boyhood friends, Wing, an Ojibwa Indian, and Jesse, from Medora, North Dakota, the young men travel across country by horseback, train, and stagecoach on their journey to join the Rough Riders and Theodore Roosevelt. This book is the story of their journey, the training of the troops, and the war in Cuba. It is a coming-of-age tale of bravery, courage, hardships and patriotism set against the background of emergence of the U.S.A. as a world power. Nivek's dispatches to the **Minnesota News** give a personal account of the times. *201 pages – author illustrated*